For Anna —
With great
respect for
all of your
work on
Death, Sex,
+ Money.

Caryn

Heaven in Your Bones

by Caryn Daus Flanagan with Illustrations by Kelly Halpin

Ordering information at www.carynflanagan.com.

For Katy and Sarah in loving memory of Ellen and Alan Daus.

Proceeds from the sale of this book will be donated to ACCESS, a nonprofit providing
emotional support resources and services for people who have lost loved ones in aircraft accidents.

www.accesshelp.org

Grief support for people affected by air disasters

*"Nothing compares to the comfort and care
of talking to someone who's been there"*

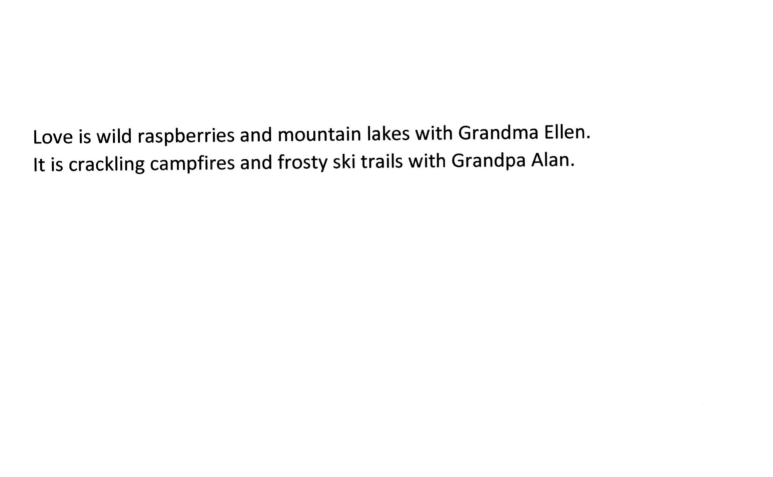

Love is wild raspberries and mountain lakes with Grandma Ellen.
It is crackling campfires and frosty ski trails with Grandpa Alan.

Love is bubbly bath time, giggly stories, and tuck-ins with Mommy and Daddy.
Love is family, and family makes my heart full.

Dark time, nighttime.
Late night phone ring-rings.

Morning's hushed voices are tucked behind doors.

Something is different.
Something unknown.
I feel small and kind of afraid.

There is sad and terrible news.

A small airplane, cloudy mountains, and our grandparents are gone.
They have gone to Heaven.

No more forest exploring with Grandma Ellen.
No more ski runs with Grandpa Alan.

I hear the clock tick-tocking on the bookshelf. Mommy pulls me super close and strokes my hair. A tear trickles off her cheek and down the back of my neck. I feel empty inside.

Where is Heaven?
Why did they go there?
Will we ever see them again?

I have lots of questions.

Dinging doorbells, ringing phones.

All day long friends bring flowers and hugs and covered dishes. Mrs. Rauch pulls me into her perfumey neck and slobbers in my ear, "Oh Sarah, such a dreadful loss."

Everything makes my head hurt so I go to my room and hide under the covers.

Did we really lose *Grandma Ellen and Grandpa Alan?*
Where did they go?
Can we go find *them?*

Katy finds me in my room.

She crawls into my bed and snuggles deep. Her weight feels like sadness. I try tickling her neck to make her feel better, but it just makes her mad and she stomps out of my room.

Daddy comes in to check on me.

Says they loved me very much.

Says they will always be watching over me from Heaven.

"But where *is* Heaven?" my voice asks.

He says a whole bunch of words that don't make sense.

That all grandparents go to Heaven.
That they are a part of me.
That they will always be with me.

But how can that be if they are lost *and* gone?

Everything is so confusing. I tuck back under my pillow so I can think harder.

All that thinking makes me sleepy. I wake up alone, covered with my favorite blanket. No dinging doorbells. No ringing phones.

I pad out to the living room where the last rays of sun stretch my shadow long across the room. I find Mommy and Daddy sitting close on the couch. The only sound is the clock, still tick-tocking on the bookshelf.

"I have a question," I say.

"Next time we go to the lake, will Grandma Ellen be able to see the sunset with me?"

Daddy nods, "She will."

Tick-tock goes the clock while I think a little more.

"And will Grandpa Alan watch me chase the butterflies?"

"He certainly will," Mommy says with a tiny smile.

I feel a little less empty inside.

Nighttime, hushed house time.
I find Mommy alone in her room, tissues scattered.

"Mommy, I have another question."

I take a deep breath.

"Is Heaven in your *bones*?"

She doesn't say anything for a long time. She just looks at me.

"Yes. Absolutely," she says. "Heaven is in your bones."
She shines a big smile and hugs me tight.
I think she feels a little less empty inside, too.

Outside is dark, but stars brighten the sky.
I realize things are different now, and that makes me sad.

But then I think about love.

Love is still here.
So are wild raspberries and splashy mountain lakes.
Next winter there will be snow-covered ski trails.
And next summer there will be butterflies to chase.

And I know that even without Grandma Ellen and Grandpa Alan,
we will always be a family.

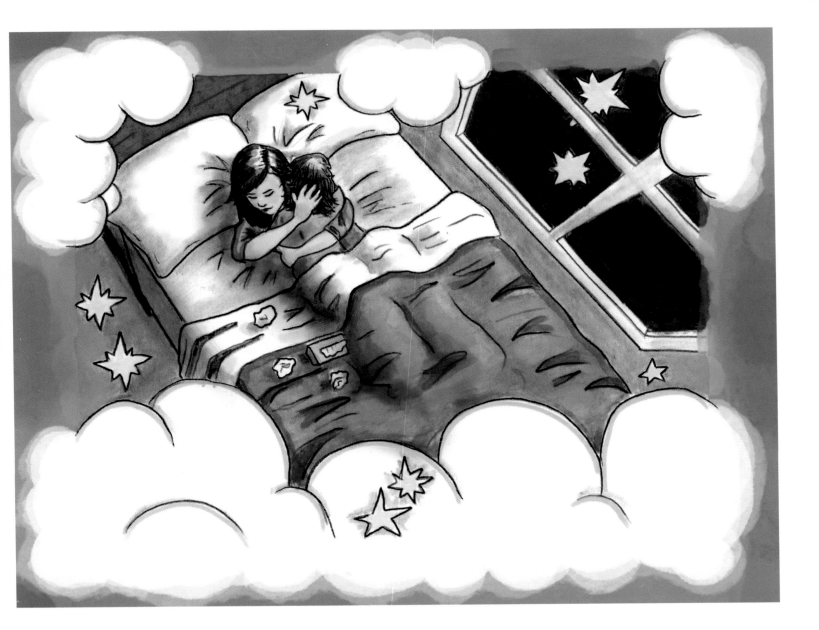